leapfrog

Rhyme Time

Woolly the Bully

First published in 2007 by
Franklin Watts
338 Euston Road
London
NW1 3BH

Franklin Watts Australia
Level 17/207 Kent Street
Sydney
NSW 2000

Text © Sue Graves 2007
Illustration © Tim Archbold 2007

The rights of Sue Graves to be identified as the author
and Tim Archbold as the illustrator of this Work have
been asserted in accordance with the Copyright, Designs
and Patents Act, 1988.

A CIP catalogue record for this book is available
from the British Library.

ISBN 978 0 7496 7098 6 (hbk)
ISBN 978 0 7496 7790 9 (pbk)

Series Editor: Jackie Hamley
Editor: Melanie Palmer
Series Advisor: Dr Barrie Wade
Series Designer: Peter Scoulding

Printed in China

Franklin Watts is a division of
Hachette Children's Books,
an Hachette Livre UK company.

Woolly the Bully

by Sue Graves

Illustrated by Tim Archbold

W
FRANKLIN WATTS
LONDON•SYDNEY

Woolly was a mammoth.
He was Rocky's
favourite pet.

But Woolly was a bully –
the worst that you can get.

He tripped up Mrs Pebble,
and made her spill the tea.

Then he frightened
Mr Pebble ...

Grrr!

and chased him up a tree!

Mr and Mrs Pebble
saw Rocky and his dad.

"We don't want bullies

here," they said.

"He'll have to go.
He's bad!"

So sadly Rocky and his dad
sent Woolly on his way.

But Woolly hid behind
the cave.

He hoped that he could stay.

Later on there was
a thunderstorm.

It rained and rained
all night.

The rain filled up
the Pebbles'
cave.

It was a scary sight!

"HELP, HELP!" yelled
Mrs Pebble.

"We're stuck on a water spout!"

Woolly heard them yelling.
He ran to get them out.

"Thanks Woolly," said
Mr Pebble. "Please don't
go away."

"We'd like you here
forever. Please say
that you will stay."

Now Woolly's back with
Rocky. He's still his
favourite pet.

Woolly never bullies now.
He's the best pet you
can get!

Welcome
back Woolly

Leapfrog has been specially designed to fit the requirements of the National Literacy Strategy. It offers real books for beginning readers by top authors and illustrators. There are 67 Leapfrog stories to choose from:

The Bossy Cockerel
ISBN 978 0 7496 3828 3

Bill's Baggy Trousers
ISBN 978 0 7496 3829 0

Little Joe's Big Race
ISBN 978 0 7496 3832 0

The Little Star
ISBN 978 0 7496 3833 7

The Cheeky Monkey
ISBN 978 0 7496 3830 6

Selfish Sophie
ISBN 978 0 7496 4385 0

Recycled!
ISBN 978 0 7496 4388 1

Felix on the Move
ISBN 978 0 7496 4387 4

Pippa and Poppa
ISBN 978 0 7496 4386 7

Jack's Party
ISBN 978 0 7496 4389 8

The Best Snowman
ISBN 978 0 7496 4390 4

Mary and the Fairy
ISBN 978 0 7496 4633 2

The Crying Princess
ISBN 978 0 7496 4632 5

Jasper and Jess
ISBN 978 0 7496 4081 1

The Lazy Scarecrow
ISBN 978 0 7496 4082 8

The Naughty Puppy
ISBN 978 0 7496 4383 6

Big Bad Blob
ISBN 978 0 7496 7092 4*
ISBN 978 0 7496 7796 1

Cara's Breakfast
ISBN 978 0 7496 7093 1*
ISBN 978 0 7496 7797 8

Why Not?
ISBN 978 0 7496 7094 8*
ISBN 978 0 7496 7798 5

Croc's Tooth
ISBN 978 0 7496 7095 5*
ISBN 978 0 7496 7799 2

The Magic Word
ISBN 978 0 7496 7096 2*
ISBN 978 0 7496 7800 5

Tim's Tent
ISBN 978 0 7496 7097 9*
ISBN 978 0 7496 7801 2

FAIRY TALES

Cinderella
ISBN 978 0 7496 4228 0

The Three Little Pigs
ISBN 978 0 7496 4227 3

Jack and the Beanstalk
ISBN 978 0 7496 4229 7

The Three Billy Goats Gruff
ISBN 978 0 7496 4226 6

Goldilocks and the Three Bears
ISBN 978 0 7496 4225 9

Little Red Riding Hood
ISBN 978 0 7496 4224 2

Rapunzel
ISBN 978 0 7496 6159 5

Snow White
ISBN 978 0 7496 6161 8

The Emperor's New Clothes
ISBN 978 0 7496 6163 2

The Pied Piper of Hamelin
ISBN 978 0 7496 6164 9

Hansel and Gretel
ISBN 978 0 7496 6162 5

The Sleeping Beauty
ISBN 978 0 7496 6160 1

Rumpelstiltskin
ISBN 978 0 7496 6165 6

The Ugly Duckling
ISBN 978 0 7496 6166 3

Puss in Boots
ISBN 978 0 7496 6167 0

The Frog Prince
ISBN 978 0 7496 6168 7

The Princess and the Pea
ISBN 978 0 7496 6169 4

Dick Whittington
ISBN 978 0 7496 6170 0

The Elves and the Shoemaker
ISBN 978 0 7496 6581 4

The Little Match Girl
ISBN 978 0 7496 6582 1

The Little Mermaid
ISBN 978 0 7496 6583 8

The Little Red Hen
ISBN 978 0 7496 6585 2

The Nightingale
ISBN 978 0 7496 6586 9

Thumbelina
ISBN 978 0 7496 6587 6

RHYME TIME

Mr Spotty's Potty
ISBN 978 0 7496 3831 3

Eight Enormous Elephants
ISBN 978 0 7496 4634 9

Freddie's Fears
ISBN 978 0 7496 4382 9

Squeaky Clean
ISBN 978 0 7496 6805 1

Craig's Crocodile
ISBN 978 0 7496 6806 8

Felicity Floss: Tooth Fairy
ISBN 978 0 7496 6807 5

Captain Cool
ISBN 978 0 7496 6808 2

Monster Cake
ISBN 978 0 7496 6809 9

The Super Trolley Ride
ISBN 978 0 7496 6810 5

The Royal Jumble Sale
ISBN 978 0 7496 6811 2

But, Mum!
ISBN 978 0 7496 6812 9

Dan's Gran's Goat
ISBN 978 0 7496 6814 3

Lighthouse Mouse
ISBN 978 0 7496 6815 0

Big Bad Bart
ISBN 978 0 7496 6816 7

Ron's Race
ISBN 978 0 7496 6817 4

Woolly the Bully
ISBN 978 0 7496 7098 6*
ISBN 978 0 7496 7790 9

Boris the Spider
ISBN 978 0 7496 7099 3*
ISBN 978 0 7496 7791 6

Miss Polly's Seaside Brolly
ISBN 978 0 7496 7100 6*
ISBN 978 0 7496 7792 3

The Lonely Pirate
ISBN 978 0 7496 7101 3*
ISBN 978 0 7496 7793 0

What a Frog!
ISBN 978 0 7496 7102 0*
ISBN 978 0 7496 7794 7

Juggling Joe
ISBN 978 0 7496 7103 7*
ISBN 978 0 7496 7795 4

* hardback